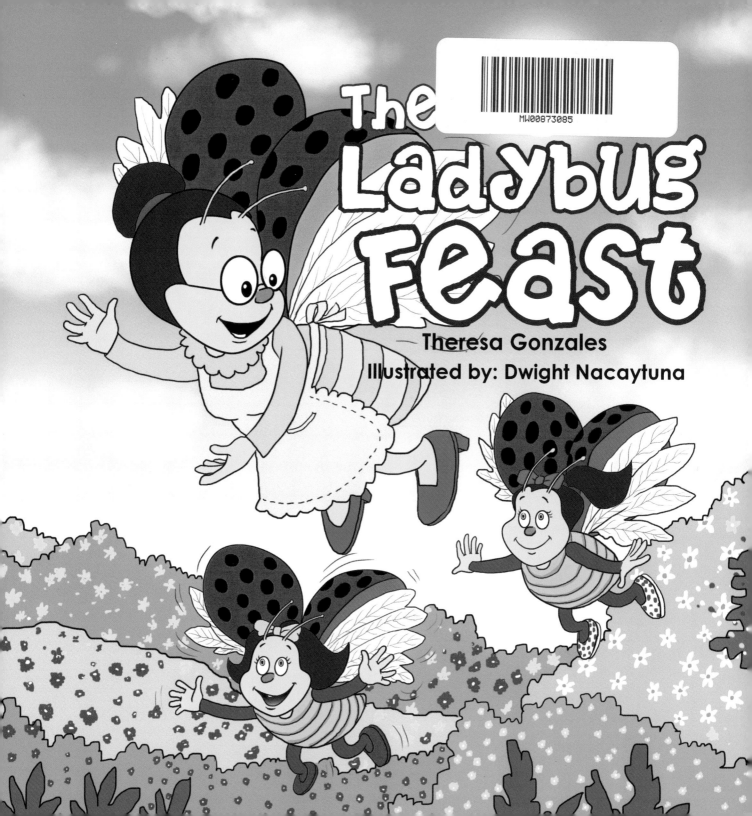

The Ladybug Feast

Theresa Gonzales

Illustrated by: Dwight Nacaytuna

ISBN: Softcover   978-1-5434-1618-3
        Hardcover   978-1-5434-1619-0
        EBook   978-1-5434-1617-6

Print information available on the last page

Rev. date: 05/04/2017

To order additional copies of this book, contact:
Xlibris
1-888-795-4274
www.Xlibris.com
Orders@Xlibris.com

DEDICATION

This book is dedicated to my daughter Amy (1972-2013), my guardian angel. Her humor, can do attitude, and kindness inspires me each and every day.

To my friends and family whose unconditional love and support gave me strength to get through the darkest time of my life.

ACKNOWLEDGMENT

I would like to acknowledge my nephew, Tony Segura, who encouraged me to turn my stories into books for children. His experience and enthusiasm made me realize that he should be involved in this process as my creative collaborator!

Momma Ladybug and her two daughters, Penelope and Priscilla live in the flower garden on a great big flower leaf. It was early in the morning and Momma Ladybug went to wake up Penelope and Priscilla.

"Wake up girls, it is time to get up! up! up! wake up!" said Momma Ladybug. As Penelope and Priscilla woke up rubbing their little eyes and stretching their little wings, they both said "we're hungry!"

"Get up, there are plenty of little bug mites ready to be eaten!" said Momma Ladybug. "Oh Momma, said Penelope sighing; "I don't want to eat bug mites. We have bug mites for breakfast, lunch, and dinner!"

"Yah Momma, we want to eat cookies, watermelon, and potato chips like Ralphie the fly gets to eat!" shouted Priscilla. "Well, that is very nice for Ralphie the fly, but you are ladybugs and what is the duty of every good Ladybug?" she asked.

As they rolled their eyes sighing with a deep breath, they answered, "we know Momma, rid the flower gardens of pesky little bug mites so people can have wonderful, beautiful flower gardens that they can be proud of."

"That is right," encouraged Momma Ladybug; "that is what we were put on this Earth for, we are very important and we must never forget what our duty is. Now let's get going girls, we have a lot to do! All you have to do is use your imagination. Bug mites can taste like anything you want them to. My favorite are chocolate bug mites."

"But Momma, bug mites just taste like … well bug mites right?" Penelope questioned. "Oh no my dear, not if you use your imagination. Now off with you both, shoo fly away!"

Penelope and Priscilla looked at each other and just rolled their eyes, lifted their wings and flew away into the flower garden looking back at Momma Ladybug and was still wondering what she meant.

Penelope swooped down on a big purple hollyhock flower and grabbed up a bug mite, popped it in her mouth, rolled it around, and thought to herself, "yummy, this little bug mite tastes just like a sweet cherry!" "Priscilla, Priscilla!" Penelope shouted, "it is true, Momma Ladybug was right, use your imagination. I just ate the sweetest red cherry!"

"What! Have you gone crazy too?" Priscilla shook her head questionably. "It works, just close your eyes and imagine you are eating something really special!" shouted Penelope, and then she flew around popping more bug mites into her mouth. "Ok, here I go." Priscilla swooped down on a wonderful orange lily and popped a bug mite into her mouth. She imagined she was eating something sweet and crunchy. With a content smile on her face, she said "Oh the joy of using your imagination!"

Penelope and Priscilla spent the day eating all the wonderful imaginary foods they had always wondered about and by the end of the day they were so full and satisfied they could hardly fly home to their big leaf in the garden.

As the sun went down and the stars came up, Penelope and Priscilla laid down on their leaf with their tummies bulging and their little wings spread out. They could only imagine what feast was in store for them when they woke up in the morning. They closed their eyes and fell fast asleep.

The End

CPSIA information can be obtained
at www.ICGtesting.com
Printed in the USA
LVIC04n2043021217
558425LV00018B/318